Benjamin's Portrait

Copyright © 1986 by Alan Baker. First published in
1986 in Great Britain by Andre Deutsch Limited.

Printed in Hong Kong

First Edition
1 2 3 4 5 6 7 8 9 10

Library of Congress Cataloging in Publication Data

    Baker, Alan.
      Benjamin's portrait.

      Summary: Benjamin the hamster tries to paint his
portrait with some unexpected results.
      [1. Hamsters — Fiction.   2. Painting — Fiction.
3. Humorous — stories] I. Title.
PZ7.B1688Bi 1987   [E]   86-10396
ISBN 0-688-06877-4
ISBN 0-688-06878-2 (lib. bdg.)

Benjamin's Portrait

Story and pictures by

ALAN BAKER

Lothrop, Lee
& Shepard Books
New York

ANIMAL PORTRAIT GALLERY

The ears are good but I don't like the eyes.

That's brilliant.

Ah! That's what I call a handsome beast.

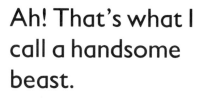

Why don't I paint myself? It looks quite easy.

Paint, canvas, water, brush...now it's up to me.

First a pencil sketch.

Now to brighten it up.

I'll just get the lid off. Ah! Powder paint.

Ahhhchooo…

Powder's too messy…I'll try tubes.

Oh dear. What a mess!

I'd better clean myself up.

Paws first.

Whoops! Help!

I hate being wet.

Can't do any more till I've got myself dry.

That's better.

Now back to work.
It's a pretty good
likeness already.

A little black here
and...it's perfect. I'll just check
the details in the mirror.

A hamster shouldn't
look like a baboon.

There must be an easier way to get a perfect likeness.

Photography…I shouldn't have any trouble with that.
Just hold steady and…Click!